Dinosaur Pals
First Day Friends

by Pat Brigandi • illustrations by Maine Diaz

It's Monday morning!
Happy students arrive at Dino School.
"Hi, Ty," shouted Kayla. "Look. I found some pretty flowers
for show and tell."
"I have a rocket," said Ty. "I made it myself!"

"I brought my new backpack," exclaimed Addy.
"I brought a new board game
that I got for my birthday," added Max.

The kindergarten students were ready
to share their things in class.

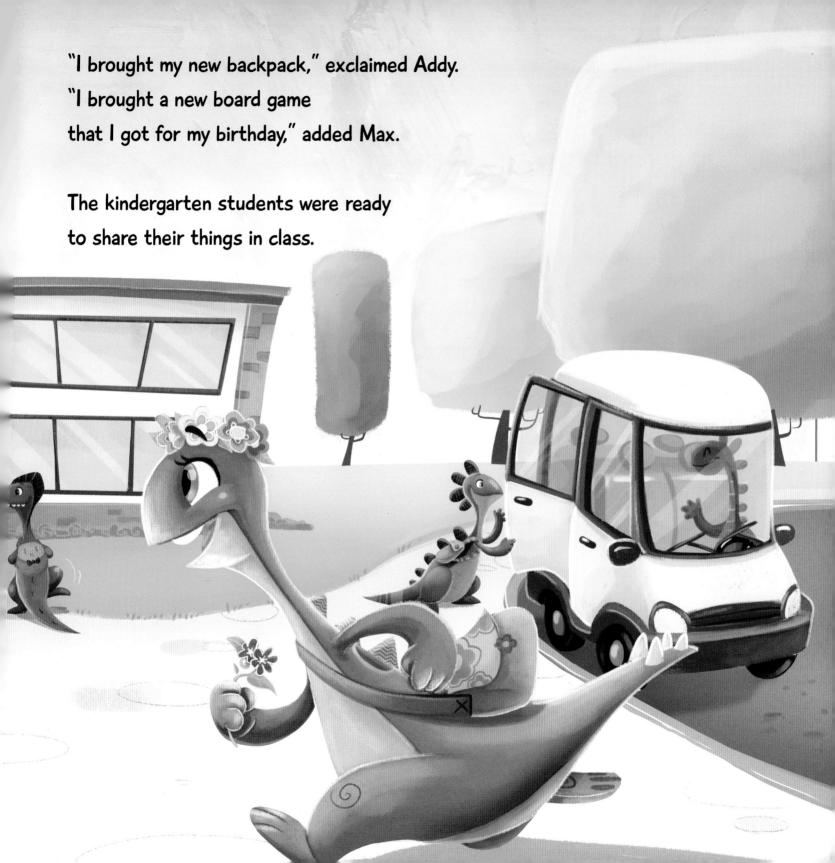

"Good morning, children!"
greeted their teacher, Mrs. Gronk.
"Good morning, Mrs. Gronk!"
said Ty, Kayla, Addy, and Max.

"I have a surprise for you," said Mrs. Gronk. "You're getting a new classmate today! His name is Kevin." "Yay!" they all cheered.

The new student came with his dad.
"Come on, Kev. It's your first day here,
and we're late," said his dad.
"I don't want to stay!" said Kevin.
He started to cry.

In the classroom, Mrs. Gronk started
Morning Meeting with the students.
She was about to ask a question.
Suddenly Ty shouted, "Mrs. Gronk,
there's someone at the door."
All the students stared.

"EVERYONE is looking at me,"
Kevin whispered to his dad.
"Everything will be all right, son,"
his dad said quietly.
"I think you're really going to like it here."
Kevin sniffled and wiped away a tear.

Mrs. Gronk quickly stepped to the door.
"Come in," she said. "I'm Mrs. Gronk,
and this must be Kevin."
"I'm so sorry we're late. I got lost,"
Mr. Spinosaurus explained.

"Class, say hi to Kevin," said Mrs. Gronk.
"Hi, Kevin!" they all shouted.
Kevin just sniffled and stared at the floor.

Everyone tried to cheer Kevin up.

"Come on, Kev!" Ty smiled.

"Let's put your backpack in your cubby."

And they did.

"Let's do this puzzle together, Kev," said Max.
And they did.

Kayla showed Kevin the nature corner.

"We planted seeds and we're watching them grow," she explained.

"Let's water the plants together!"

And they did.

Addy showed Kevin the reading corner.
"Do you have a favorite book?" she asked.
Kevin pointed. "That one," he said.
"Let's all read it together," smiled Mrs. Gronk.
And they did.

Kevin was still sad.

Ty raced to the bricks and block corner.
"Come on, Kev," said Ty. "We'll have fun!"
"Okay," whispered Kevin.
"Ty!" cried Mrs. Gronk. "No running, please!"

Too late.

CRASH! BANG! PLOP!

Ty ran right into a pile of blocks
and fell to the floor!

THUD!

"Oh my!" cried Mrs. Gronk. "Are you okay?"

Ty nodded.

"Class, help him clean up the mess," said Mrs. Gronk.

Suddenly Max started laughing.

"Ty, that was so funny!" Max said.

Ty laughed along with Max.

Then Kayla and Addy started laughing.

Now Kevin was laughing, too!

"Okay, class. Let's settle down," said Mrs. Gronk.
"Why don't all of you build something together?"

And they did.

"We made the best castle ever!"
said Kevin with a big smile.

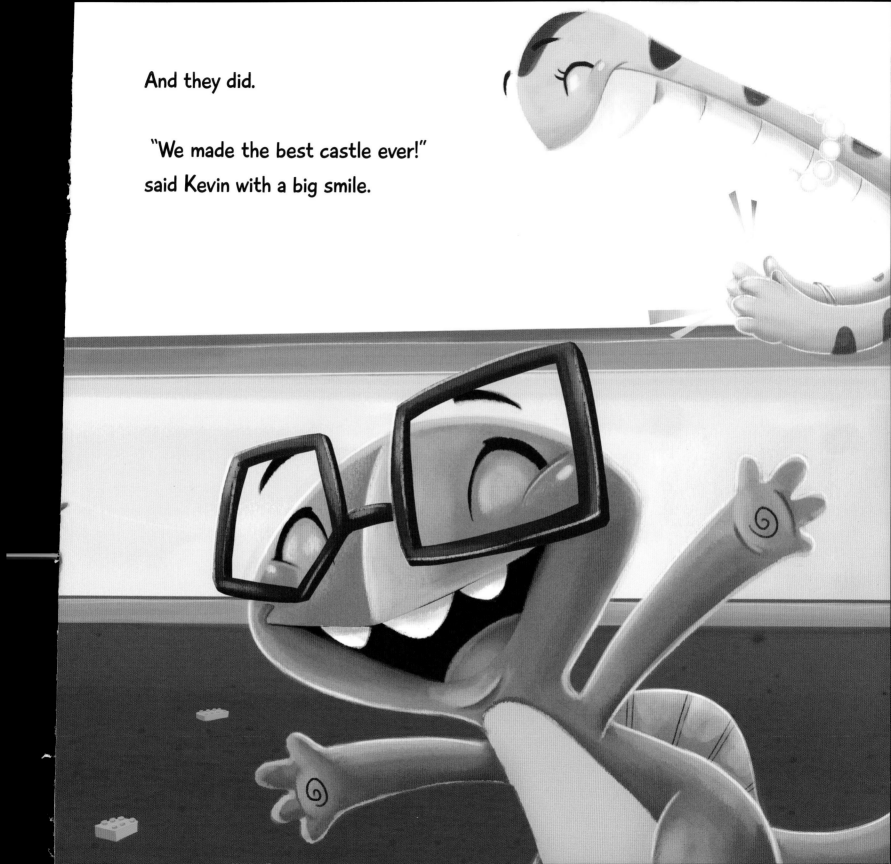

At last, the class began show-and-tell time.
Kayla shared her pretty flowers.
Ty showed off his new rocket.
Addy let everyone hold her backpack.
"It's big enough to carry all my library books,"
she said proudly.
Max showed the class how to
play his new board game.

"I don't have anything to show," Kevin whispered.

"Well, you can tell us something!" said Ty.

"Yeah!" they all cried.

"Okay," said Kevin. "I can tell a riddle.
What kind of ship is the best ship?"

No one could guess the answer.

"We give up," said Addy.

"It's FRIENDSHIP!" Kevin said smiling.
Everyone cheered and laughed along with Kevin.

New school. New friends.
Kevin's first day in kindergarten
was a good day after all!